Guinea Pigs
Don't Read Books

GUINEA PIGS DON'T READ BOOKS

Colleen Stanley Bare

PHOTOGRAPHS BY THE AUTHOR

Dodd, Mead & Company   New York

To Michelle

Text copyright © 1985 by Colleen Stanley Bare
Photographs copyright © 1985 by Colleen Stanley Bare
All rights reserved
No part of this book may be reproduced in any form
without permission in writing from the publisher
Distributed in Canada by
McClelland and Stewart Limited, Toronto
Printed in Hong Kong by South China Printing Company
1 2 3 4 5 6 7 8 9 10

Library of Congress Cataloging in Publication Data

Bare, Colleen Stanley.
Guinea pigs don't read books.

Summary: Points out that though guinea pigs
don't read books or play checkers, they make
good friends and are gentle and lovable.
 1. Guinea pigs as pets — Juvenile literature.
[1. Guinea pigs] I. Title.
SF459.G9B37 1985   636'.93234   84-18707
ISBN 0-396-08538-5

Book shown in jacket photograph is *ABC*
by Helen Federico © 1969, 1963
by Western Publishing Company, Inc.
Reprinted by permission

Guinea pigs don't read books, count numbers, run computers,

play checkers, or watch TV, but there are other things they do.

They chew, and chew, and chew.
Foods like apples, celery, carrots,

and if you don't watch out, they'll chew your toys.

Guinea pigs see well
and stare at you.

They hear well
and listen.

They smell well
and sniff and sniff.

Guinea pigs make sounds.
They growl, grunt, gurgle,
purr, squeal, whistle,
and squeak,
squeak,
squeak.

Guinea pigs don't wear hats,
but they do wear fur coats.

Short, soft smooth ones

rough, bristly ones

long, silky ones.

Their coats come in many colors.

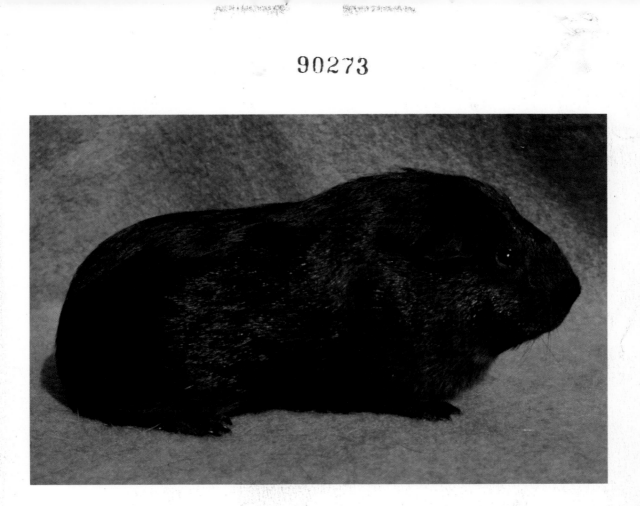

Blue, beige, cream,
red, orange, lilac,
chocolate, white, black.

And in mixtures of colors.

Guinea pigs aren't pigs.
They don't eat like pigs,
       walk like pigs,
       sound like pigs.
Even baby guinea pigs
don't look like baby pigs.

Guinea pigs like to be held
and hugged.
They are gentle
and calm
and lovable.

Guinea pigs may not
read books,
but they can be your
friends.